W9-AUS-100

Paddy Pig's
Poems

Paddy Pig's
Poems

*A Story About an Amusing Fellow and
His Friends*

by DONALD CHARLES

SIMON AND SCHUSTER BOOKS
FOR YOUNG READERS
Published by Simon & Schuster Inc., New York

SIMON AND SCHUSTER BOOKS FOR YOUNG READERS
Simon and Schuster Building, Rockefeller Center, 1230 Avenue of the Americas, New York, New York 10020
Copyright © 1989 by Donald Charles   All rights reserved including the right of reproduction
in whole or in part in any form. SIMON AND SCHUSTER BOOKS FOR YOUNG READERS is a trademark of
Simon & Schuster Inc.   Typography by Mary Ahern   Manufactured in the United States of America

10   9   8   7   6   5   4   3   2   1

Library of Congress Cataloging-in-Publication Data   Charles, Donald. Paddy Pig's Poems: the story of
an amusing fellow and his friends / by Donald Charles. p. cm.
SUMMARY: Extraordinary Victorian poet
Paddy Pig, has an unusual way of ending his poems that his friends fail to appreciate.
ISBN 0-671-67081-6 [1. Pigs–Fiction. 2. Friendship–Fiction.]   I. Title.
PZ7.C374Pad 1989   [E]–dc19
88-12094   CIP   AC

For Shirley and her little pal

Paddy Pig sent notes to his friends, Bertie
Bunny and Dilly Dog:

> *Please join my poetry club, and see*
> *What a fine afternoon can be.*
> *We'll read poems by you and me,*
> *So be here Monday at half-past four.*

Monday afternoon, Bertie and Dilly arrived at Paddy Pig's house.

"If we met at half-past *three*," said Bertie, "Your invitation would have ended with a rhyme."

"I wouldn't have been ready then," Paddy said. "In fact, I must go next door and borrow a chair." And Paddy excused himself and left the room.

"Poor Paddy Pig," sighed Bertie. "He writes the worst poems ever!"

"And now he wants to start a *poetry* club," said Dilly, "Really!"

"Listen to this pitiful poem," Bertie said. He picked up a paper from Paddy's desk and read:

> The poems I write
> Are a real delight.
> So, please be polite
> When the rhyme is not perfect.

"He means *right*," laughed Dilly.

"Wait," Bertie snickered, "Here are some more":

> An *elephant's nose*
> Looked like a hose.
> In the garden he chose
> To pick a red zinnia.

Bertie and Dilly looked at each other and grinned.
"He should have written *a red rose*, of course,"
added Bertie.

Bertie read another poem out loud.

> On a soft summer breeze,
> A mouse smelled some cheese.
> He fell to his knees
> And cried, "Give me some, for heaven's sake!"

"Oh, *please!*" exclaimed Dilly.

"This one doesn't quite rhyme either," Bertie said.

Pigs are not neat.
When it comes to a treat,
They do like to eat
With their hands and their toes.

"Not *toes*, *feet!*" Dilly shouted gleefully.

Bertie picked up another of Paddy's poems.
"Listen to this," he said.

> If you are feeling blue
> Because you can not find your shoe,
> I will find it, that is true,
> And I will give it back to someone.

Dilly started to laugh. "Read some more," she begged.

"All right," Bertie said. "Here's one about me."

> On a day warm and sunny,
> Bertie the bunny,
> Thought it was funny
> To spread bread with peanut butter.

"He should have said *honey*," hooted Dilly.
"Is there a poem about me?"

"Yes," Bertie chuckled, and he read:

Dilly keeps a bone
By her telephone.
She's often known
To eat all by herself.

"*All alone*," Dilly cried. Bertie and Dilly
held on to one another and shook with mirth.

"His verse gets worse," Bertie giggled, pleased with himself. "Listen to this":

> *When the moon is in the sky,*
> *It makes me think of pumpkin pie.*
> *In fact, no matter how I try,*
> *I think of food: I wonder about that.*

Just then Paddy Pig came into the room carrying
a chair. "Are you laughing at my poems?" he asked
softly as he sat down.

"Well, really," Bertie sniffed, "Your poems don't have
proper endings."

"I'm sure you can't help it," added Dilly smugly.

"I suppose you can do better," Paddy said.

"Oh yes," said Bertie. "The last line should always rhyme."

"Of course," agreed Dilly.

"Now here is the right way to rhyme a poem," Bertie said. "I wrote it myself." He cleared his throat.

> Paddy's poems are never long:
> They start out sounding like a song,
> But, just when they are going strong,
> They end up sounding very wrong.

"I see," Paddy Pig replied, "But I like surprise endings. For example, this is my latest poem." Then Paddy read:

> When rude friends ask why
> There's a tear in my eye,
> I just want to cry
> "Hello and farewell!"

Bertie and Dilly could not help but smile. "You mean *goodbye*!" they shouted in unison.

"*Goodbye!*" said Paddy Pig, as he showed them to the door.

"I think that was a proper ending," he said to himself. And he sat down to write another poem.

DATE DUE